Cherry City Kitty

ISBN 978-0-578-52324-8

Printed in the United States of America

Cherry City Kitty

Written by
Donna Rubin

Illustrated by
Maranda Chavez

Traverse City, Michigan
2019

Dedicated to the two men in my life, my father and my husband, for always believing in me. Their unending love helped me harvest this sweet book; the fruit of my labor.

-Donna

Dedicated to my son Ruben Miles for the sweet snuggles and wiggles he gave me while I worked on every page.

-Maranda

I'm the Cherry City Kitty, now wouldn't it be a pity to miss any of the sweet treats Traverse City has to share.

Miss Pitty Pat's Cherry Pies

cherries

pies

dessert

I'm Miss Pitty Pat, a kitty cat lucky enough to live in Traverse City, Michigan…the cherry capital of the world. Come along with me to taste the many treats found at our National Cherry Festival, learn how our famous tart cherries are grown and harvested, plus try a few yummy recipes made with Michigan cherries, of course. I think you'll agree that this beautiful bay area along Lake Michigan is the cat's meow.

When we reach the end of my **tail**, it will be as clear as our crystal blue waters surrounded by two peninsulas*, that this kitty's cherry city is the place to be. *Look at the glossary in the back for bushels of "**cherrylicious**" terms like this.

Traverse City

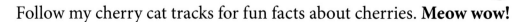

Follow my cherry cat tracks for fun facts about cherries. **Meow wow!**

Cherries discovered in a Turkish cave from 70 B.C. reveal the fruit was native* to Asia. Romans, Greeks and Chinese cooked with cherries many centuries ago.

Producing over 250 million pounds every year makes Michigan the number one tart cherry producer in the United States. Our sour Montmorency variety is prized for pies, jam and juice. Sweet Bing and Morello cherries are **purrfect** for eating fresh, dried or frozen. Maraschino cherries are the bright red balls of fruit that kids of all ages enjoy atop ice cream sundaes. This pussycat loves ice cream of any kind…with a cherry on top, pretty please.

Try this no-bake recipe made with Michigan cherries.
Pawse and always ask an adult to help you in the kitchen.

Miss Pitty Pat's Cherry Chocolate Protein Balls

½ cup dried Michigan tart cherries coarsely chopped
1 cup old fashioned rolled oats
1 cup shredded coconut
½ cup peanut butter or nut free substitute
½ cup mini chocolate chips
1/3 cup Michigan honey
1 teaspoon vanilla extract

Mix all ingredients in a bowl. Chill 30 minutes in a refrigerator.
Roll into small balls. Keep in an airtight container up to 1 week
for a high energy after school snack.

I'm the Cherry City Kitty, now wouldn't it be a pity to miss some of the history that Traverse City has to share.

Miss Pitty Pat's Cherry Pies

cherries

pies

dessert

Cherry cat track fact...

Cherries were first introduced to North America by English colonists*. President Thomas Jefferson grew sour cherries in his orchard at Monticello. Did you ever hear the legend of young George Washington chopping down his father's cherry tree? Just like our first President, I cannot tell a lie either. **Meow wow!**

The almost 4 million cherry trees found in northern Michigan today trace back to 1852 when a missionary* planted the first cherry orchard on Old Mission peninsula. Reverend Doughtery and his Native American neighbors were amazed how well the trees survived in the sandy soil beside Lake Michigan. Little did they know that nearby lake waters warmed harsh winter wind and cooled hot summer air to make the **purrfect** growing temperatures for cherries.

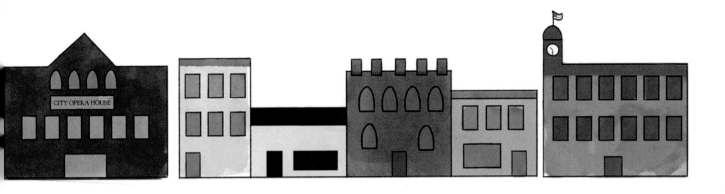

Cherries belong to the stone fruit* family, like peaches, plums and apricots. An average tree makes enough fruit for 70 pies in one season. Growing fruit for about 30 years, a single cherry tree could produce over 2,000 pies in its lifetime. Of course pie isn't the only reason to grow cherries, but it certainly is a mighty fine one. In 1988 the fine folks in Traverse City baked the world's largest cherry pie measuring 18 feet across. The giant pie pan is still on view in our quaint little town.

World's
Largest Pie
1988

Cherry cat track fact...

My great grand kitty once made an enormous pie for the president of the United States to celebrate the 1926 Cherry Festival. It was 3 feet in diameter*, weighed 42 pounds and contained 5,000 cherries. I'll bet President Calvin Coolidge looked like a real fat cat after sampling that gigantic cherry pie.

I'm the Cherry City Kitty, now wouldn't it be a pity to miss the four seasons Traverse City has to share.

Miss Pitty Pat's Cherry Pies

cherries

pies

dessert

Cherry cat track fact...

Once handpicked by workers on ladders, tart cherries are now shaken off trees by machines and kept in cold water until they are canned, dried or frozen. At summer roadside stands Traverse area farmers let visitors traipse* into their orchards to pick warm, juicy sweet cherries and enjoy them fresh off the trees.

Each season is important for growing cherries. During winter, trees lie dormant*
through the snowy season. They need cold Michigan winters in order to
germinate*. In spring, rolling hills explode in pink and white blossoms. Farmers
release bees in their orchards to pollinate* clusters of blooms that ripen into
bunches of cherries.

Summer months finds farmers working long hours to collect fresh ripe cherries at their peak. After the harvest, autumn's cooler temperatures turn leaves a radiant reddish-orange before falling to the ground and signaling cherry trees to take a long winter's nap.

Cherry harvests happen quickly to keep the fruit bright eyed and bushy tailed like me. Trucks with shakers work the orchards day and night. A robotic arm shakes the trunk so thousands of cherries tumble gently onto a soft conveyor* system that helps clean and sort cherries on site. They are chilled immediately in cold water since firm cherries are easiest to pit before being canned, frozen or dried at local factories.

Purrhaps you would like to grow your own cherry tree.
If your climate* is similar to ours up north, you should be able to.

1. Eat some unrefrigerated cherries from a local farmer and save the pits.
2. Soak the pits in warm water for five minutes then wipe off any clinging fruit.
3. Spread pits on paper towels and dry for 5 days.
4. Keep pits in a tight fitting plastic container until ready to plant.
5. On a warm fall day, plant several seeds two inches deep and one foot apart.
6. In the spring, seedlings will sprout…then just wait for those luscious cherries.

After all that hard work growing your own cherries,
cool off with this nutritious smoothie.

Cherry City Smoothie

½ cup frozen sweet or sour Michigan cherries
½ cup vanilla Greek or regular yogurt
½ cup milk
½ cup ice cubes

Place all ingredients in blender and whirl until smooth.
Pour and enjoy with a straw.

Miss Pitty Pat likes to blend sweet cherries with Greek yogurt and sour cherries
with regular yogurt. Try your own combinations to tickle your taste buds.

I'm the Cherry City Kitty, now wouldn't it be a pity
to miss any of the fun the Cherry Festival has to share.

Miss Pitty Pat's
Cherry Pies

cherries

pies

dessert

Cherry cat track fact...

In 1925 Traverse City farmers began a tradition* called the Blessing of the Blossoms.
They asked local churches to pray for a good cherry crop during a one-day picnic and parade.
The ceremony brought such great results, it continues to this very day known as the
National Cherry Festival.

The National Cherry Festival has grown throughout the decades* from brass bands and marching contests of the 1920s to local beauty queens on floats in the 1930s. Currently, in its tenth decade, the festival combines our hometown fun of parades with carnival rides and all things **cherrylicious** to sip, slurp and savor at the midway.

Our July celebration now brings a half million folks from everywhere to enjoy old-fashioned fun at over 150 family friendly events. From pie eating and pit spitting contests to bicycle rodeos and nightly outdoor concerts, there is a bushel of fun for everyone. Even pets get to vie* for prizes at the pet show. I do not care to enter the fattest cat contest, but I know a few dogs to nominate* for the ugliest mutt prize. **Grr.**

With over 100 free events during the annual Cherry Festival, kids of all ages feel like life is just a bowl of cherries. Take a glance at some yummy summer fun.

Heritage Day Pow Wow

Fireworks

Cherry Orchard Tours

Big Wheels & Bike Races

Bubble Gum Blowing Contest

Pit Spitting Contest

Chalk Art Contest

Ultimate Air Dog Contest

Sandcastle Contest

Classic Car Show

Kids' Club Games

Turtle Races

Life is just a bowl of...

Cherry cat track fact...

Our local Coast Guard hosts the National Cherry Festival Airshow.
Demonstration teams execute aerial* displays and high-speed stunts.
Meow wow! They make my fur stand on end!

I'm the Cherry City Kitty, now wouldn't it be a pity to miss any benefits that cherries have to share.

Miss Pitty Pat's Cherry Pies

cherries

pies

dessert

Cherry cat track fact...

Several studies suggest health benefits of tart cherries. Dried or fresh cherries or cherry juice may ease muscle pain and encourage sleep. Miss Pitty Pat has never experienced any trouble taking catnaps. Thanks, cherries!

Now folks, the Cherry Festival isn't the only place to find cherry treats. More than 200 cherry products are sold all over the world. Bite into our ruby red morsels* inside chocolate covered cherries, cherry fudge, snack mixes, preserves, salsas and barbeque sauces, just to name a few. You can even find cherries in burgers or brats, beverages, ice cream and delicious dessert pizza. We are so cherry crazy in Michigan, there is no telling what will be next…I'm wondering about cherry cat snacks or dog treats. Mmm.

Try this deliciously easy cherry recipe, but ask an adult for help in the kitchen.

Cherry City Kitty's Purrfect Cherry Crumble

Filling:
3 cups frozen tart cherries, thawed and drained
¼ cup sugar
2 Tablespoons corn starch
1/8 teaspoon almond or vanilla extract

Crumble:
¾ cup brown sugar
½ cup flour
½ cup granola
1/3 cup cold butter cut into small pieces
1 teaspoon cinnamon

Preheat oven to 375 degrees.
Grease an 8x8 inch square pan.
Toss filling ingredients in a bowl and pour into pan.
Blend crumble ingredients with a fork in another bowl 'til it looks crumbly.
Sprinkle over filling and bake 30 minutes until brown.
Serve with cherry vanilla ice cream…Miss Pitty Pat's favorite topping!

I'm the Cherry City Kitty, now wouldn't it be a pity if we missed other treasures Northern Michigan has to share.

Miss Pitty Pat's Cherry Pies

cherries

pies

dessert

Well, well, where do I start? When I get an itch in my tail to travel there are so many places in northern Michigan to visit. You might enjoy water more than a kitty cat like me, so try water skiing or tubing, kayaks, canoes or sailing. If you would rather keep your fur dry, enjoy nearby golf courses, bike along the Tart Trail and visit local lighthouses and museums.

Cherry cat track fact...

Once voted the most beautiful spot in America, Sleeping Bear Dunes* National Lakeshore is a must see and a must climb for everyone. Padding across the three and a half mile sandy trek* heats my paws so I dip them in the crystal clear waters of Lake Michigan. A **purrfect** day at the dazzling dunes ends with stargazing and story telling around a campfire. Zzz! Sleeping Cat Dunes, get it?

Spring and summer aren't the only seasons for finding fun around here. Autumn brings spectacular colors to admire while going on old-fashioned hayrides or apple and pumpkin picking at local farms. Winter weather never slows down anyone either; ski slopes and cross-country trails are always busy. Horse drawn sleigh rides and authentic dog sleds abound. 'Sure glad no one ever thought of cat sleds. Everyone knows herding cats won't work!

I'm the Cherry City Kitty, now wouldn't it be a pity to leave Traverse City without a plan to return.

Up North

Well, friends, I hope you've enjoyed our time together up north and learned fascinating facts about cherries. It has tickled my whiskers to spend time with you sharing why my cherry city is the cat's pajamas. But don't take my word for it; just come back anytime to savor all the sights, sounds and sweet treats you can find near the tip of our marvelous Michigan mitten.

Wait, I have one more recipe to share. It's named after our Cherry Royale Parade held during the festival. If you ask this cream loving kitty, it sure takes the cake.

No Bake Cherry Royale Mini Cheesecakes

12 cupcake liners and cupcake tin
12 vanilla wafer cookies

2 cups nondairy whipped topping
2 bricks of cream cheese softened (8 ounces each)
¾ cup powdered sugar
1 tsp vanilla
½ tsp lemon juice

1 jar cherry pie filling

Spray 12 cupcake liners placed in cupcake tin with non stick cooking spray.
Place 1 cookie in each liner.

Beat softened cream cheese, vanilla, lemon juice and powdered sugar until smooth.
Gently fold in the whipped topping with a rubber spatula.

Spoon over cookies and chill in fridge for 4 hours or freeze for 2 hours.

Top with cherry pie filling and serve.

Glossary

 aerial: happening in the air

colonists: inhabitants of the 13 British colonies that made the U.S.A.

conveyor: a system that moves products from one place to another

decade: a span of ten years

diameter: the distance from side to side, through the center

dormant: not active but able to become active

dune: a hill of sand formed by the wind

germinate: when seeds grow into plants

missionary: a person sent to an area to do religious work

morsel: a small piece of food

native: born or grown in a particular place

nominate: to name for an honor or award

peninsula: a piece of land surrounded by water on 3 sides

pollinate: to spread pollen from one plant to another for growing

processor: a machine or company that prepares something

stone fruit: a fruit with a single, hard seed in the center

tradition: something handed down by generations

traipse: to walk or move casually

trek: a journey or a trip

vie: to compete

About the Author

Donna Rubin loves all things Michigan…so much so that she and her husband have recently retired to Traverse City. They live their best life on a local lake with their trained therapy dog Pax. Donna and Pax volunteer to read to children at local libraries and bookstores with their Miss Pitty Pat puppet. Contact for author visits with this or her first book, Apple Cider Pup, at **donnarubin1@me.com**

About the Illustrator

Maranda Chavez is a cartoonist that resides in Lansing Michigan. Because she has a passion for animals, her home has many fuzzy, scaley, and slimey companions. After enjoying local shops and beautiful Michigan weather with her family, nothing beats a cat nap with her rescue kitty Rocket. **#artbymaranda**

Made in the USA
Middletown, DE
30 September 2019